The Clumsy Cow

ReadZone Books Limited

50 Godfrey Avenue
Twickenham
TW2 7PF
UK

For my siblings, you know why

First published in this edition 2014

© in this edition ReadZone Books Limited 2014
© in text Julia Moffatt 2004
© in illustrations Lisa Williams 2004

Julia Moffatt has asserted her right under the Copyright Designs
and Patents Act 1988 to be identified as the author of this work.

Lisa Williams has asserted her right under the Copyright Designs
and Patents Act 1988 to be identified as the illustrator of this work.

British Library Cataloguing in Publication Data (CIP) is available
for this title.

Printed in Malta by Melita Press

ISBN 978 1 78322 157 8

Visit our website: www.readzonebooks.com

The Clumsy Cow

by Julia Moffatt

illustrated by Lisa Williams

READZONE

Buttercup the cow was very clumsy.

5

When the farmer milked her, she knocked the bucket over.

"Oops-a-daisy," said Buttercup.

8

9

Buttercup went for a walk.

On the way she met a hen.

"Hello," she said.

Then Buttercup
slipped and...

...trod on the nest and broke some eggs.

"Oops-a-daisy,"
said Buttercup.

Buttercup was hungry.
She ran to get her lunch...

...but she bumped into all the other cows.

18

"Oops-a-daisy," said Buttercup.

None of the animals
wanted Buttercup
near them.

"I wish I wasn't so clumsy," cried Buttercup.

One night, Buttercup heard a noise in the hen house.

23

"Cluck, cluck!" cried the hens.

24

she fell on top of
a big fox!

"Hurray for Buttercup!" shouted the animals.

"Oops-a-daisy," smiled Buttercup.

31

Did you enjoy this book?

Look out for more *Magpies* titles –
fun stories in 150 words

The Clumsy Cow by Julia Moffat and Lisa Williams
ISBN 978 1 78322 157 8

The Disappearing Cheese by Paul Harrison and Ruth Rivers
ISBN 978 1 78322 470 8

Flying South by Alan Durant and Kath Lucas
ISBN 978 1 78322 410 4

Fred and Finn by Madeline Goodey and Mike Gordon
ISBN 978 1 78322 411 1

Growl! by Vivian French and Tim Archbold
ISBN 978 1 78322 412 8

I wish I was an Alien by Vivian French and Lisa Williams
ISBN 978 1 78322 413 5

Lovely, lovely Pirate Gold by Scoular Anderson
ISBN 978 1 78322 206 3

Pet to School Day by Hilary Robinson and Tim Archbold
ISBN 978 1 78322 471 5

Tall Tilly by Jillian Powell and Tim Archbold
ISBN 978 1 78322 414 2

Terry the Flying Turtle by Anna Wilson and Mike Gordon
ISBN 978 1 78322 415 9

Too Small by Kay Woodward and Deborah van de Leijgraaf
ISBN 978 1 78322 156 1

Turn off the Telly by Charlie Gardner and Barbara Nascimbeni
ISBN 978 1 78322 158 5